King Claude in Central Park

written by
Donna Saccone Pinamonti

illustrated by
Rebecca McSherry

To my father, Philip, who loved New York City and its parks, and who taught me the value of hard work and volunteering to make a difference in this world.

Book Vine Press
2516 Highland Dr.
Palatine, IL 60067

King Claude's a talking Shih Tzu, golden brown.

He was named for the vet who lived across town.

He lived with his loving family;

Bryan, Michelle, Mom and Daddy.

King Claude and the kids were ready for their trip.
The basket was packed with food and drinks to sip.
They were going to go to New York City,
to see Central Park, which was so pretty.

All around the park, they always loved to run.
Climbing rocks and hiking trails was so much fun!

Michelle loved the fountains and pretty flowers
and climbing up Belvedere Castle Towers.

"Let's go see all of the statues," said Michelle.

They loved Hans Christian Andersen, his books were swell.

They climbed atop Alice in Wonderland.

The mushroom was huge; White Rabbit was grand.

Bryan was so happy to go to the Boathouse
and watch model boats, like Stuart Little, the mouse.

But King Claude led the way to his favorite place
to see Balto, the rescue dog, who ran a fast pace.

It was time to stop for a delicious lunch.

There was so much food to munch and crunch.

They spread out their blanket and all had their fill,

then King Claude and the kids climbed up the big hill.

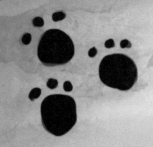

The family walked all through Central Park,
but the sky was getting a little dark.
"Hey look," said Michelle, "I can see the big lake."
"There are rowboats," said Bryan, "that we can take!"

Dad said, "Let's all go for a ride in a boat."
So into the rowboat they climbed for a float.
By bridges they sailed, looking at buildings so high.
When they passed by the ducks, they took off to fly.

They rowed across the lake, sailing by willows.
The clouds up above looked like big, black pillows.

"Row faster," said Mom. "We must beat the rain."
"We can't," yelled the kids, "Our arms are in pain."

King Claude said, "You can do it, please just try,"
and perhaps that is the reason why ...
They paddled very fast across the lake,
as thunder boomed and their lives were at stake.

They all made it safely, back to the dock,
then they ran to take shelter by a big rock.
Though it was too late and they were already wet,
this exciting day was not quite over yet.

Off they went on a horse and carriage ride.
King Claude sat up in front, beaming with pride.

They rode through Central Park, looking at all they had seen
and they all agreed this day had been just like a dream.
This great day had come to a perfect end
King Claude said, "I hope we come back again!"

King Claude with author,
Donna S. Pinamonti, in the rowboat.

King Claude after getting
caught in the rainstorm.

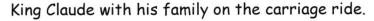

King Claude with his family on the carriage ride.

King Claude keeping score of the
game on the picnic blanket.

Can you find King Claude in Central Park?

About the Author and Illustrator

Donna Saccone Pinamonti was a first grade teacher for over fifteen years. Upon retirement, her love of children, reading, and her dog, Claude, inspired her to begin a new career as an author of children's books. She is thrilled to team up with a former student to create this picture book series about the adventures of her two children and their dog. She is proud of her first published book, "King Claude the Talking Dog" and is excited for the publication of the next books in the series. Donna loves photography and travel, and lives in Middletown, New Jersey.

Rebecca McSherry has been practicing art from the moment she could pick up a pencil. Before attending college, she studied fine arts and worked at "Inspired Minds," where she gained artistic skills that she still uses today. She is currently attending Pennsylvania State University as a graphic design major. She hopes to work in any field involving illustration or animation. Rebecca is more than excited to help create a wonderful book series with her first grade teacher.

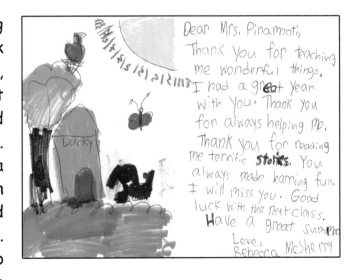

CPSIA information can be obtained
at www.ICGtesting.com
Printed in the USA
BVHW020304171221
624169BV00002B/8